P9-DID-852

*To the Fabulous Foos:*
*Here's to many happy years*
*of bopping field mice*
*on the head*
*—F. N. B.*

*For my mother*
*—G. B. K.*

Atheneum Books for Young Readers
An imprint of Simon & Schuster Children's
Publishing Division
1230 Avenue of the Americas
New York, New York 10020
Text copyright © 2008 by Franny Billingsley
Illustrations copyright © 2008 by G. Brian Karas
Book design by Ann Bobco
The text for this book is set in Golden Cockerel.
The illustrations for this book are rendered in
gouache and acrylic with pencil.
Manufactured in China
First Edition
10 9 8 7 6 5 4 3 2 1
Library of Congress Cataloging-in-Publication Data
Billingsley, Franny, 1954–
Big Bad Bunny / Franny Billingsley ;
illustrated by G. Brian Karas. —1st ed.
p.  cm.
"A Richard Jackson book."
Summary: When Baby Boo-Boo, a mouse dressed
in a bunny suit, becomes lost in the forest, her
mother follows the sound of her cries to locate her.
ISBN-13: 978-1-4169-0601-8
ISBN-10: 1-4169-0601-0
[1. Mice—Fiction. 2. Mother and child—Fiction.]
I. Karas, G. Brian, ill.  II. Title.
PZ7.B4985Big 2008
[E]—dc22
2006032754

# Big Bad Bunny

STORY BY FRANNY BILLINGSLEY

ART BY
G. BRIAN KARAS

A Richard Jackson Book • Atheneum Books for Young Readers • New York London Toronto Sydney

Big Bad Bunny has long sharp claws.

Scritch!

Scritch!

Scritch!

But over in the Mouse House, everything is quiet. It's naptime, and Mama Mouse tucks her babies into bed.

Mama Mouse kisses Little Tippy.

"I love you, Little Tippy, and I always will."

Mama Mouse kisses Little Flurry.
"I love you, Little Flurry, and I always will."

Big Bad Bunny comes to a mucky swamp.
Does that stop Big Bad Bunny?
No!
Big Bad Bunny can go anywhere.

Splat!

Mama Mouse kisses . . .
But wait!
Where is Baby Boo-Boo?

Eek!

Mama Mouse races into the forest.

Big Bad Bunny comes to thick, tangly bushes.
Does that stop Big Bad Bunny?
No!
Big Bad Bunny can go anywhere.

Mama Mouse comes to a rushing stream.

Does that stop Mama Mouse?

No!

Mama Mouse will go anywhere for Baby Boo-Boo.

*Splish!*

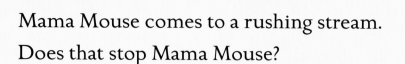

# "BABY?!"

## GRRRR. STOMP. ROAR.

What's that noise?

It's Big Bad Bunny howling as loud
as a hungry hyena.

## "HERE ARE MY LONG SHARP CLAWS!"

# Scritch!

Mama Mouse comes to a mucky swamp.

Does that stop Mama Mouse?

No!

Mama Mouse will go anywhere for Baby Boo-Boo.

*Squoozle!*

Baby!

Where are you, Baby?

# "BABY?!"

## GRRRR. STOMP. ROAR.

What's that noise?

It's Big Bad Bunny howling as loud as ten hungry hyenas

### "HERE ARE MY POINTY YELLOW TEETH!"

Mama Mouse comes to thick, tangly bushes.

Does that stop Mama Mouse?

No!

Mama Mouse will go anywhere for Baby Boo-Boo.

*Pitter-pat!*

Baby!

# "BABY?!"
## GRRRR. STOMP. ROAR.
What's that noise?
It's Big Bad Bunny howling
as loud as . . .

But wait!
Big Bad Bunny has come to a hill.
It's a steep, slippery hill.
Does that stop Big Bad Bunny?

**Yes!**

**Big Bad Bunny is lost!**

Eek! Eek! Eek! Eek! Eek! Eek

Mama Mouse stops.

Mama Mouse listens.

What's that noise?

It's her own Baby Boo-Boo howling as loud as a hundred hungry hyenas.

*k!*

*Eek!*

"Boo-Boo! My own Baby Boo-Boo!
At last I found you!"

"I'm not Baby Boo-Boo!" Big Bad Bunny wipes her eyes.
"Oh?" says Mama Mouse.
"I'm not a baby!" Big Bad Bunny sniffles.
"You're not?" says Mama Mouse.

Big Bad Bunny howls as loud
as a thousand hungry hyenas.

"I'm Big Bad Bunny!"

"Oh!" says Mama Mouse.

"Nice to meet you. Do you want to go home?"

Big Bad Bunny holds Mama Mouse's paw.

They come to the thick,
tangly bushes.
*Pitter-pat!*
**Crash!**

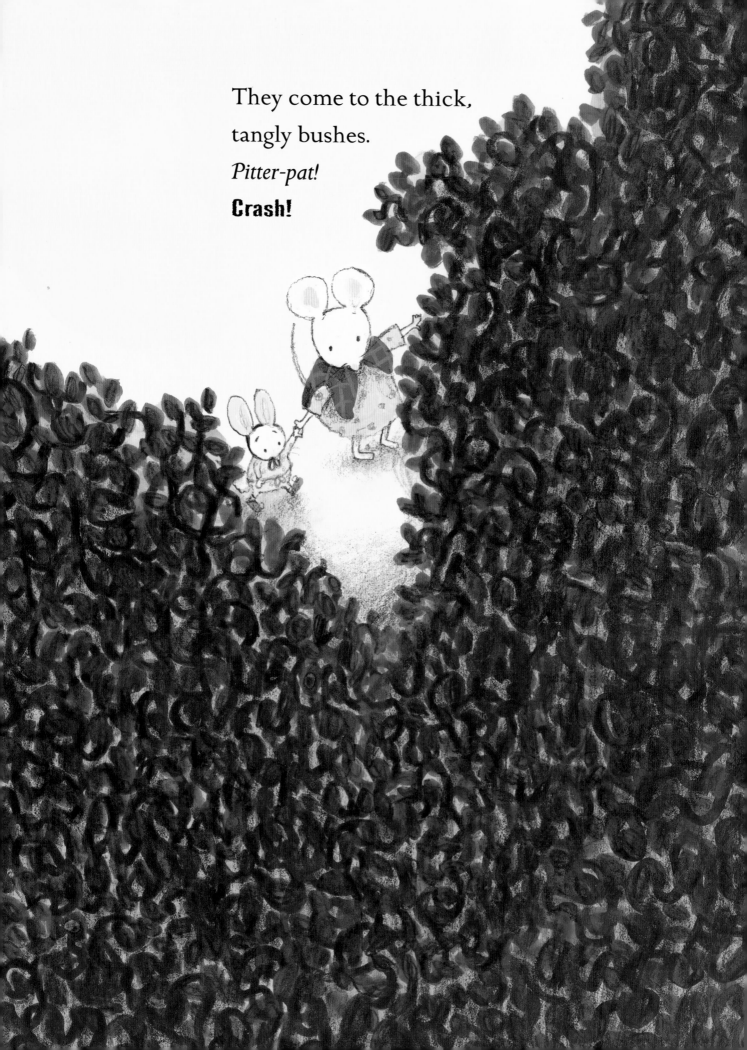

They come to the mucky swamp.

*Squoozle!*

**Splat!**

They come to the rushing stream.
*Splish!*
**Ka-splosh!**

They come to the Mouse House.

*Tiptoe!*

**Tiptoe!**

Mama Mouse tucks
Big Bad Bunny into bed.

"I love you, Big Bad Bunny, and I always will."